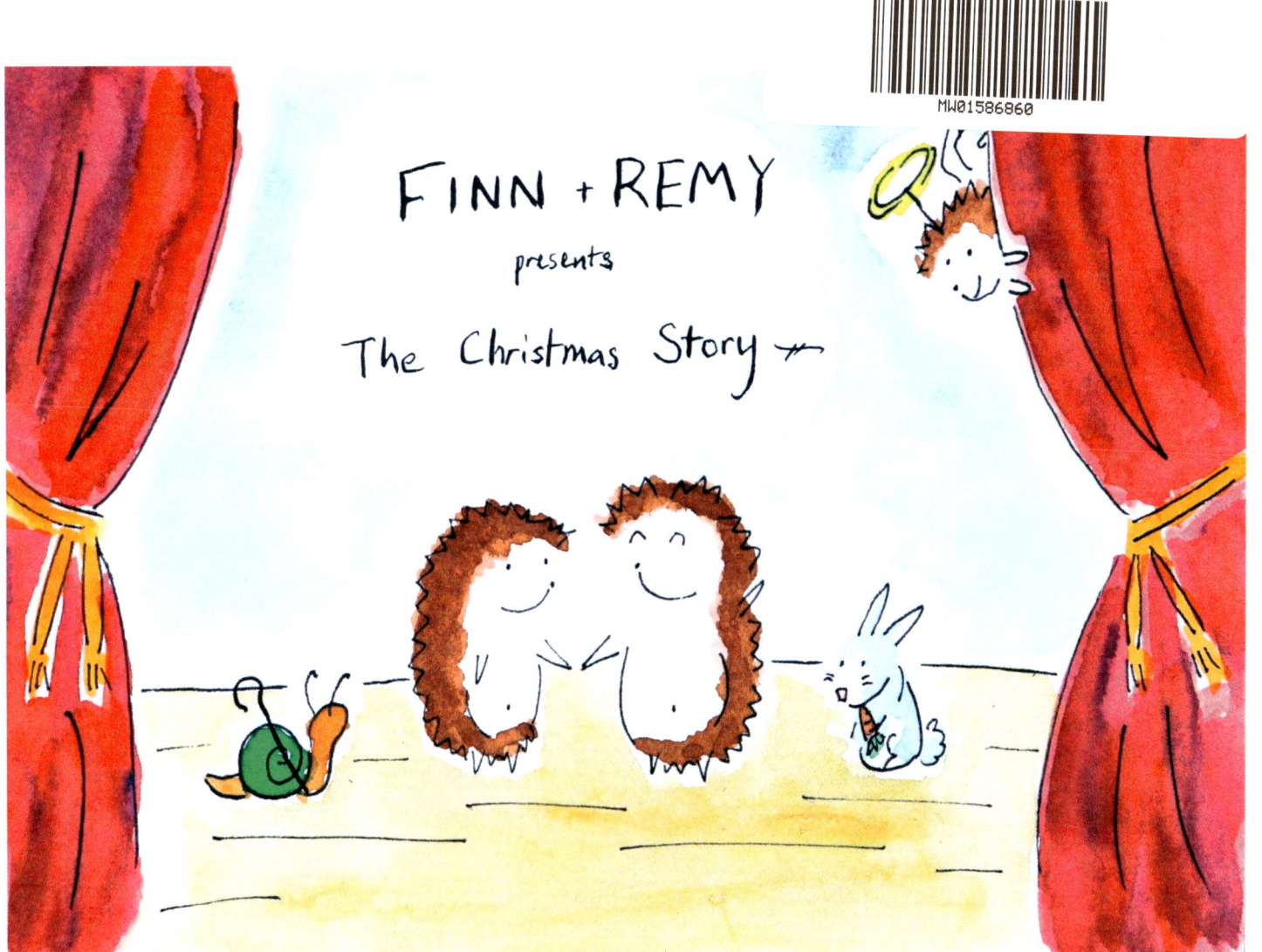

Want to go backstage with Finn and Remy and see how each illustration was drawn? Just go to www.finnandremy.com to watch the "making of" every picture in this book. Grab some paint and follow along. All of the time-lapse videos are completely free!

— Jane

For more Finn and Remy, check out www.finnandremy.com

Copyright © 2017 Jane Du

No part of this book may be reproduced by any means without permission in writing from the author.

A long, long time ago, there was a young man named Joseph and a young lady named Mary. They were betrothed, which means they planned to get married soon.

Mary and Joseph lived in the land of Galilee, in a town called Nazareth, where Joseph worked as a carpenter. They didn't know it yet, but their lives were about to change forever.

One evening, while Mary was out walking, an angel named Gabriel appeared in the sky. Gabriel told Mary that she would soon become pregnant with a baby named Jesus, and that Jesus would be the son of God.

Mary was very excited to hear this news, but when she told Joseph, he was very confused. Mary tried to explain that she was chosen by God to bring His son into the world, but Joseph did not understand.

When Gabriel spoke to Mary, he also told Mary to visit her cousin Elizabeth because she had a big surprise. So, Mary decided to go and stay with Elizabeth for a while. Elizabeth was so happy to see Mary and welcomed Mary into her home.

Elizabeth was much older and everyone knew she could not have children. But Elizabeth told Mary a secret: the angel Gabriel also came to her family and now Elizabeth was pregnant with a baby named John.

Back in Nazareth, an angel visited Joseph in a dream. The angel explained that Mary was very special and that she was chosen by God to have His son. And Joseph should marry her and raise the baby together.

When Mary returned home, Joseph told her that an angel appeared to him and explained everything. After that, Joseph and Mary got married and started planning to raise their family.

Around that time, the Romans were taking a census and asked every person to return to their hometown to register. Because Joseph's family were descendants from King David, Joseph had to return to the town of Bethlehem in the land of Judea.

So, even though Mary was pregnant with baby Jesus, Joseph packed up his family and they traveled to Bethlehem.

In those days, the journey to Bethlehem was long and slow. They traveled for many weeks. Mary and Joseph even had to cross the mighty Jordan River to reach their destination.

Eventually, after a long and difficult journey, Mary and Joseph arrived in the town of Bethlehem. It was getting late and, because of the census, they struggled to find a place to stay.

Mary was so tired and she told Joseph that the baby would be coming soon. But every innkeeper said that all their rooms were full. Finally, Joseph found an innkeeper who had an idea.

Even though there was no room left at the inn, there was a stable out back where the animals lived. The innkeeper said that Mary and Joseph could stay here for the night.

As Mary was very tired, Joseph agreed. They laid down with the animals and rested for a while. Not long thereafter, the baby Jesus was born. The animals all gathered around and looked at the beautiful baby.

The little bird, who was with the animals in the stable, flew out into the fields. She flew far and wide. She saw shepherds tending their flocks and told them to come to the stable for the Son of God was born.

Far away in the east, three wise men looked up into the sky. They saw a star burning more brightly than any other star they had ever seen. From their studies, they knew that the brilliant star foretold the birth of the King of Kings.

So the three wise men got on their camels and rode west. They followed the star all the way to Judea. When they arrived, they first went to see the ruler of Judea, King Herod.

The wise men told King Herod that the King of Kings was born. King Herod asked the wise men to find the baby. Then to come back and tell him so that he too may go and worship the King of Kings.

The wise men continued on until the star stopped above a little stable in Bethlehem. There, they found the baby Jesus lying in a manger. They went inside to worship him and to give him precious gifts of gold, frankincense, and myrrh.

Back in the castle, King Herod was very upset that the three wise men believed a baby could be a king over him. He ordered his guards to search Bethlehem to find the baby Jesus.

That night, an angel came to Joseph and warned him about King Herod's plan. The angel told Joseph to take Mary and the baby, to leave Bethlehem immediately, and to go somewhere safe.

So Joseph woke up Mary, packed up their things, and headed out of town with baby Jesus tucked safely in Mary's arms. They went all the way to Egypt to get away from King Herod.

Jesus lived in Egypt with his parents, Mary and Joseph, for several years until it was safe for them to go back. Then, they returned to their home in Nazareth. And that, folks, is the story of the first Christmas.

Finn and Remy live at home with their parents in Dallas, Texas. Their mom, Jane, loves to draw them as little critters and capture their shenanigans in watercolor and ink. Dad is good at keeping those shenanigans in check. You can find more Finn and Remy illustrations online at www.finnandremy.com.

Made in the USA
Monee, IL
05 December 2021

84024026R00019